MEG'S EGGS

For Katie

MEG'S EGGS

by Helen Nicoll
and Jan Pieńkowski

PUFFIN BOOKS

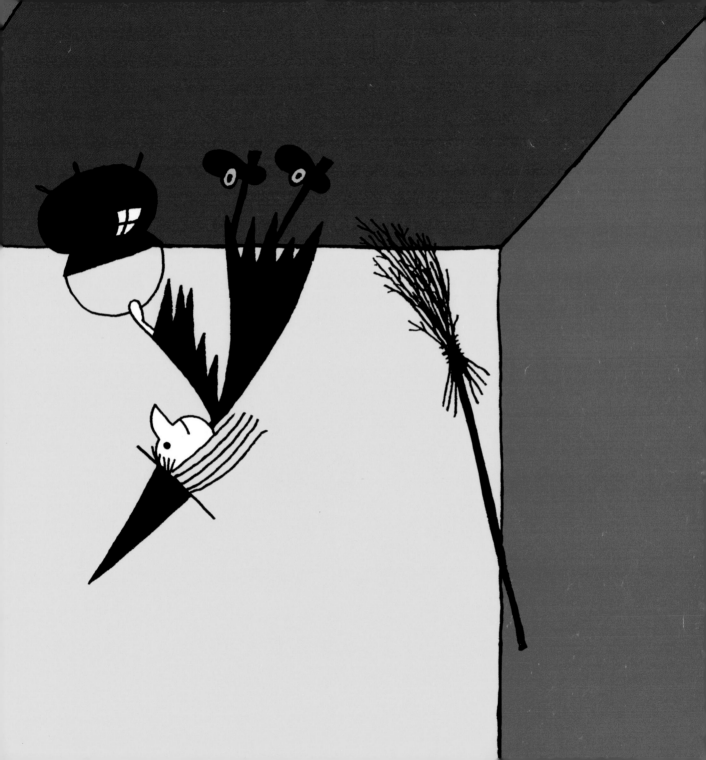

She put in
lizards, newts, 2 green frogs

PLUNK

In the middle of the night Meg heard

Meg's egg was hatching

Diplodocus was very happy

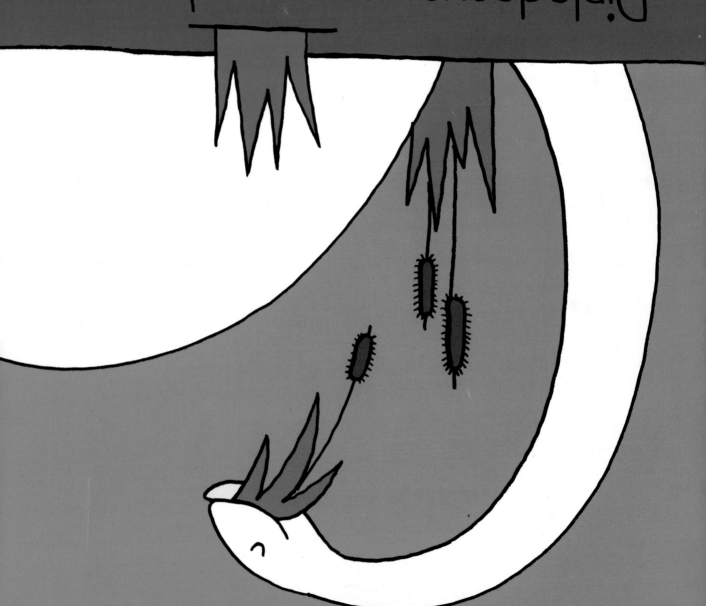

Mog was sleeping by his egg

when he heard a noise

It was another dinosaur

Mog took Stegosaurus into the garden

Owl
was
watching
the
last
egg

Out jumped Tyrannosaurus, the most ferocious of all the dinosaurs

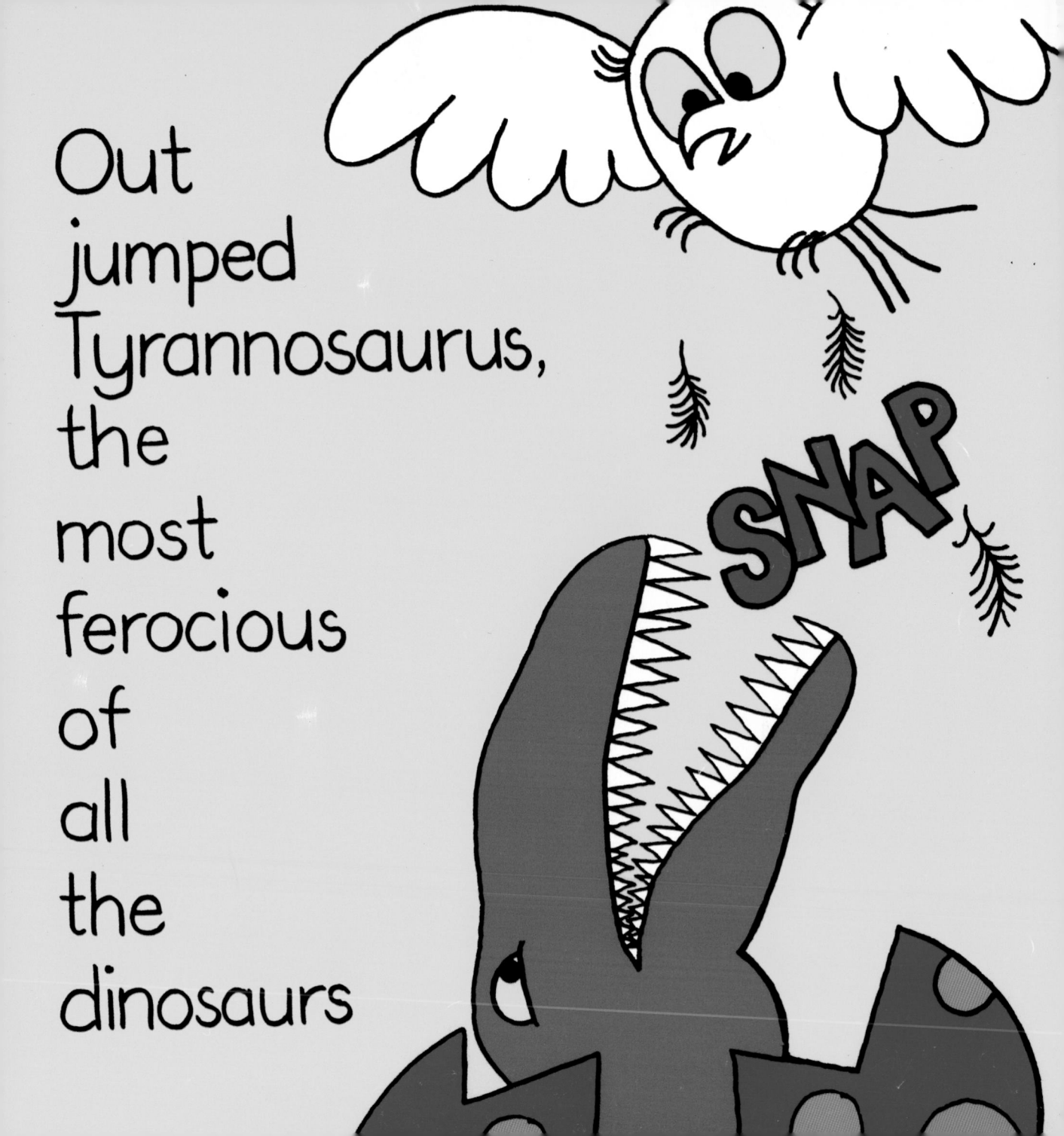

They were
very
frightened

Tyrannosaurus wanted to eat them all

Meg flew home and tried
to make a good spell

Goodbye!